Ebb & Flo

and the
Greedy Gulls

Jane Simmons

Margaret K. McElderry Books

To Celia

Margaret K. McElderry Books
An imprint of Simon & Schuster Children's Publishing Division
1230 Avenue of the Americas
New York, New York 10020

First published in Great Britain by Orchard Children's Books
First United States Edition, 2000
10 9 8 7 6 5 4 3 2 1
Printed in Singapore

Library of Congress Catalog Card Number: 99-62216
ISBN: 0-689-82484-X

It was a lovely day.
Ebb listened to the seagulls laughing.
Everything was wonderful.

Ebb closed her eyes and sniffed the sea air.
Beep, beep, said Bird.
The seagulls laughed.

Ebb snoozed on the warm sand.

The seagulls woke her.
Woof! Woof! barked Ebb.
The seagulls just laughed.

"Ebb!" said Flo. "You've eaten
all the sandwiches!"
Beep, beep, said Bird.
The seagulls laughed.

"You've eaten loads," said Flo. "Oh, Ebb!"
"Oh, Ebb!" said Mom.
Beep, beep, said Bird.
The seagulls laughed and Ebb sulked.

Ebb sulked in her favorite spot.
It was so unfair.

It began to rain. Mom and Flo
cleared the food away.
The seagulls swooped.
Waves lapped at the boat.
Ebb sulked.

"It's the seagulls! *They're* taking the food!" cried Flo.
"Shoo!" shouted Mom.
Beep, beep, said Bird.
The seagulls laughed.
Ebb sulked.

When Ebb looked up, she was all alone.
The little boat was drifting out to sea.
Woof! Woof! said Ebb. But nobody came.

The little boat started to spin.
Woof! Woof! said Ebb.
It went around
and around, faster and . . .

. . . faster and FASTER.
Woof! Woof! Woof!
barked Ebb.

CRASH!

"Where are you, Ebb?" shouted Flo.

Ebb looked up and there were Bird and Flo.
Beep, beep.
"Oh, Ebb," said Flo, "I'm sorry I blamed you."

"I do love you so much," she said.
And the seagulls laughed overhead.